Maria's Comet

Maria's

Comet

To the Students at Rosa Parks,

Follow your star!

Deborah Hopkinson

written by
DEBORAH HOPKINSON

illustrated by
DEBORAH LANINO

2014

ALADDIN PAPERBACKS
NEW YORK LONDON TORONTO SYDNEY SINGAPORE

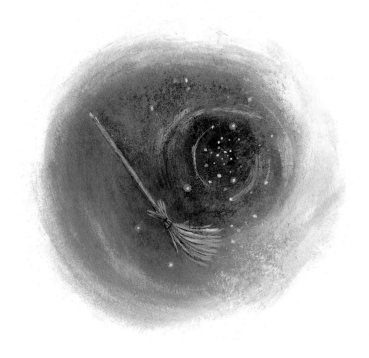

As darkness falls,

Papa goes up to the roof to sweep the sky.

When I was little,

I thought Papa stood on our rooftop

sweeping the stars into place,

with one great *whoosh* of a broom.

I was sure he swept so hard that dust flew up, higher and higher

till it scattered into a million shimmering specks above his head.

But now I'm old enough to know

Papa is an astronomer

who sweeps the sky with a small brass telescope,

moving it slowly over the sea of stars

like a sailor scanning the waves.

"A star only seems like a speck of dust

because it's so far away," Papa has told me.

"But my telescope gathers and focuses light,

to help me see each tiny point as it really is—

a giant spark of fire,

a far-off sun burning fiercely like our own."

With his telescope

Papa can find valleys and mountains on the Moon,

see stars flicker yellow, red, or deep-sea blue,

and, best of all, search for comets.

Someday, he says, we'll know what comets are made of,

but for now they are mysterious visitors,

with blurry heads and glowing tails

like ancient creatures gliding through the deep.

While Papa sweeps the sky I stay below,

pushing my straw broom to and fro.

Sometimes I stop to look out the window

and imagine the strange worlds Papa can travel

just from our silent rooftop.

If I could catch hold of a comet's tail

I'd blaze through the night sky to call on each planet:

tiny Mercury, pale Venus, and red-faced Mars,

King Jupiter, Saturn, and blue-green Uranus.

In the cold darkness far from the Sun,

I might even discover a new planet or two.

Then I'd circle warm Earth with its oceans of blue

and streak off into blackness once more.

But my world is small inside this house.

There are nine children in our family and Momma is
often tired.

So I help start the fire for breakfast,

tell my brothers and sisters bedtime stories,

and do so much mending my needle sometimes feels

as heavy as the anchor of my uncle's whaling boat.

Whenever I can, I break free from my chores.

Andrew and I climb to the attic,

spread the old atlas out upon the floor,

and imagine we're explorers in faraway lands.

Then we open Grandpa Coleman's sea chest to find

shells, scraps of silk, a single stone of jade,

and spin yarns about the fierce storms we braved

to bring our treasures home.

Our attic hideaway is a treasure trove of books, too.

Andrew likes tales about sailors best.

But I love stories of the early astronomers:

Copernicus, who tried to prove a new idea—that Earth

and all the planets circle round the Sun.

And proud Galileo, who first used telescopes to look at the sky.

Through them he discovered mountains on our Moon

and the four great moons of Jupiter.

Now Andrew wants to leave Nantucket Island

and sail away to the places we've imagined.

One night as clouds race fast across the sky,

I spy him slipping out the gate.

I chase him to the harbor, and beg for him to stay.

But he only shakes his head.

"Come with me," he says.

"Let's explore the world together."

I turn his words over and over,

like an otter trying to open an oyster shell.

And somehow when I look,

I find something wonderful and true inside.

"I *will* be an explorer," I decide.

"But I want to sail the sea of stars

and learn about the deepest space.

Maybe someday, I'll even find a comet."

By morning Andrew's whaling boat is gone.

Like so many Nantucket lads before him,

he has run away to sea.

Momma hides her tears. Papa is silent.

My little brothers and sisters cry and pull on my skirt,

till I sit them in a circle and make up stories

of all that Andrew the Sailor will see.

Then, after supper, Papa takes the whale oil lamp

and starts up to the roof.

Sometimes even a few steps can be as hard to take

as a journey to a distant land.

But now it is my turn.

So I grip the handle of my broom

and make my voice as strong as its wood.

"Let me come with you, Papa. I want to sweep the sky."

Papa stops.

Momma looks up from her sewing.

Her needle flashes silver in the firelight

as though she holds a comet in her hand.

I am afraid they will say no,

afraid they will say

a girl should only look through the eye of a sewing needle.

But perhaps they can see I need more,

and that in my heart, I have already set out.

At last Momma smiles.

"Take your cloak, Maria. The night is cool."

As I push open the door to the rooftop,

the Milky Way spreads before me

like a crazy, luminous quilt.

Each constellation is a patchwork of stories

passed down from the beginning of time—

Orion the Hunter, Taurus the Bull,

Gemini the Twins.

Each stitch is a star I want to understand—

Castor, Pollux, Rigel, and Sirius.

Papa aims the telescope and calls me over.

I'm so excited I can feel my heart pounding

but my hands are steady.

"Let's look at Polaris first," he says softly.

"It helps ships find their way because it's always north.

We call it the star of sailors."

I smile. "I wonder if Andrew is looking at it, too."

The brass telescope gleams in the darkness.

When I put my eye to it, everything else disappears.

At first I don't see anything.

Suddenly a star bursts into view.

It is only one bright spark

but it lights my heart.

It is only one star, far away.

But it seems so close

I can reach out and touch it,

I can take hold and follow,

I can go wherever it takes me.

Author's Note

"I 'swept' last night for two hours. . . . It was a grand night—not a breath of air, not a fringe of cloud, all clear, all beautiful."

—MARIA MITCHELL, 1854

Maria's Comet is a work of fiction, but it was inspired by a real person. Maria (pronounced ma-RYE-ah) Mitchell was America's first woman astronomer. Maria was born in 1818 on Nantucket Island, Massachusetts, into a large Quaker family. By day Maria worked in the Atheneum, Nantucket's public library, but at night she "swept the sky." She discovered a telescopic comet (a comet visible only through a telescope) in 1847, and in 1865 she was named the first professor of astronomy at Vassar College. Maria also helped to start the Association for the Advancement of Women and served as its president. She died in 1889.

In *Maria's Comet,* I have tried to capture Maria Mitchell's wonderful questioning spirit and dedication to women's education by showing a girl who discovers and stands up for her desire to explore the world of science. But unlike most girls of her time, the real Maria actually grew up in a family that encouraged all the children—boys *and* girls—to study science, mathematics, and astronomy. Maria's father taught her all he knew about astronomy and supported her career. Maria grew up to be a well-known scientist, but just as important, she was a dedicated teacher and mentor. Maria Mitchell was a role model and a leader at a time when many people believed women should not have careers, be scientists, or even go to college.

When Maria was a girl, only seven planets were known. Neptune was discovered during her lifetime, in 1846, but Pluto was not detected until 1930. Whenever I hear about the discoveries astronomers are making as they sweep the sky with giant telescopes and send probes to other planets, I think about Maria Mitchell. How excited she would be!

More About Astronomy Terms in This Story

Comets formed about 4.6 billion years ago, along with the Sun and planets. These "dirty snowballs" are made up of frozen gases that include water ice, with dust particles imbedded in the ice. If a comet nears the Sun, the Sun's heat evaporates some of the ice, forming a cloud of gas and dust—the comet's "head." Wind from the Sun can also blow some of this cloud into a "tail" that streams away from the Sun.

Constellations: People have always made patterns of the stars they see in the sky. These patterns, or constellations, are a little like connect-the-dot pictures. Today everyone in the world recognizes the same eighty-eight official constellations.

Nicolaus Copernicus (1473–1543): This Polish astronomer, often called the founder of modern astronomy, was one of the first to suggest Earth is a planet, and that all the planets revolve around the Sun. This was a shocking idea in his time, because people believed Earth was the center of the universe and could never move.

Galileo Galilei (1564–1642) argued so strongly that Copernicus was right about how the planets move he was put under house arrest. Galileo was the first to use a telescope for astronomy. His discoveries include the four large moons of Jupiter—Io, Europa, Ganymede, and Callisto—which we call the Galilean moons.

Stars are gaseous spheres that generate their own light. Our nearest star is the Sun, which scientists believe formed about 4.6 billion years ago. It is 100 times larger than the Earth and is made up mostly of hydrogen and some helium. On its surface the Sun is 10,000 degrees Fahrenheit, but its center is 27 million degrees! After the Sun, Sirius is the brightest star we see.

Telescope: The first telescopes were developed in the Netherlands from eyeglass lenses. In 1609 Galileo began to make and use telescopes to explore the skies. Refracting telescopes, like the one Maria and her father had, use a big lens at the front to collect and focus light. Today most telescopes are reflectors and use a curved mirror to gather and focus the light.

For Michele, who lights our lives,
and with love to Joy and family
—D. H.

To George
— D. L.

Special thanks to Dr. Katherine Bracher and Dr. Andrea Dobson, Department
of Astronomy, Whitman College; and to Patti Hanley, Mara Alper, and
Elliot Z. Levine of the Maria Mitchell Association.

First Aladdin Paperbacks edition February 2003
Text copyright © 1999 by Deborah Hopkinson
Illustrations copyright © 1999 by Deborah Lanino
ALADDIN PAPERBACKS
An imprint of Simon & Schuster
Children's Publishing Division
1230 Avenue of the Americas
New York, NY 10020

Also available in an ANNE SCHWARTZ BOOK ATHENEUM
BOOKS FOR YOUNG READERS hardcover edition.
Designed by Angela Carlino
The text of this book was set in Berkley Medium.
The illustrations are rendered in acrylic paint.
Manufactured in China
10 9 8 7 6 5 4 3 2 1

The Library of Congress has cataloged the
hardcover edition as follows:
Hopkinson, Deborah.
Maria's comet / by Deborah Hopkinson ;
Illustrated by Deborah Lanino.—1st ed.
p. cm. "An Anne Schwartz book."
Summary: As a young girl, budding astronomer
Maria Mitchell dreams of searching the night sky and
someday finding a new comet.
ISBN (hc) 0-689-81501-8
1. Mitchell, Maria, 1818-1889—Juvenile fiction.
[1. Mitchell, Maria, 1818-1889—Fiction.
2. Astronomers—Fiction. 3. Comets—Fiction.]
1. Lanino, Deborah, ill. II. Title.
PZ7.H778125Mar 1999 [E]—dc21 97-46676
ISBN (pbk.) 0-689-85678-4